To Sheena, Jordan, Danielle, and Miranda

A NOTE FROM THE AUTHOR

In his *Book of Woodcraft* the great naturalist Ernest Thompson Seton listed forty birds that he thought every child should know. Though I disagreed with some of his selections, the listing made me think: How many and which birds should every child know? Which fish? Which mammals? What other animals?

The four books in the series CRINKLEROOT'S 100 ANIMALS EVERY CHILD SHOULD KNOW (*Crinkleroot's 25 Birds, 25 Fish, 25 Mammals,* and *25 More Animals*) are intended to provide a base of knowledge of the animal kingdom. I hope my selections will make parents and teachers consider, as Mr. Seton's forty birds made me consider, which other animals should be included.

—Jim Arnosky

SIMON & SCHUSTER BOOKS FOR YOUNG READERS
An imprint of Simon & Schuster Children's Publishing Division
1230 Avenue of the Americas
New York, New York 10020
Copyright © 1993 by Jim Arnosky
All rights reserved including the right of reproduction
in whole or in part in any form.
Simon & Schuster Books for Young Readers is a trademark of Simon & Schuster

First edition
Printed in Hong Kong
10 9 8 7 6 5 4 3
The text is set in ITC Bookman Light. Typography by Julie Quan

Printed on recycled paper

LIBRARY OF CONGRESS CATALOGING-IN-PUBLICATION DATA
Arnosky, Jim.
Crinkleroot's 25 birds every child should know / by Jim Arnosky.—
1st ed.
p.   cm.
Summary: Presents the author's choices for birds with which young boys
and girls should be familiar.
ISBN 0-02-705859-X
1. Birds—Juvenile literature.   2. Birds—Identification—Juvenile
literature.   [1. Birds.]   I. Title.   II. Title: Crinkleroot's
twenty-five birds every child should know.
QL676.2.A765   1993
598—dc20   92-36059

Crinkleroot's

25 BIRDS

EVERY CHILD SHOULD KNOW

BY JIM ARNOSKY

Simon & Schuster Books for Young Readers

Hello! My name is Crinkleroot. I'm a friend to all the animals. How many animals do you know?

In this book, there are twenty-five birds you should know.

Everywhere you go, you can see birds. There are shorebirds, land birds, and water birds.

A bird's body feathers are soft and overlap to protect thoroughly against wind and rain.

In cold weather, birds keep their feathers fluffed up for better insulation.

A bird's flight feathers
are stiff and strong for pushing
hard against air.

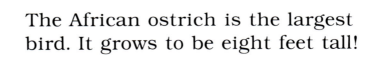

Birds fly forward by flapping
their wings up and down.

They hover by beating their
wings side to side.

Birds spread their wings
to glide and soar.

Some species of birds cannot
fly. The penguin and the ostrich are two flightless birds.

The African ostrich is the largest
bird. It grows to be eight feet tall!

Hummingbirds are the world's
smallest birds.

Have fun learning your birds!

Your friend,  Crinkleroot

Penguin

Loon

Swan

Goose

Duck

Pelican

Gull

Heron

Stork

Turkey

Chicken

Vulture

Eagle

Woodpecker

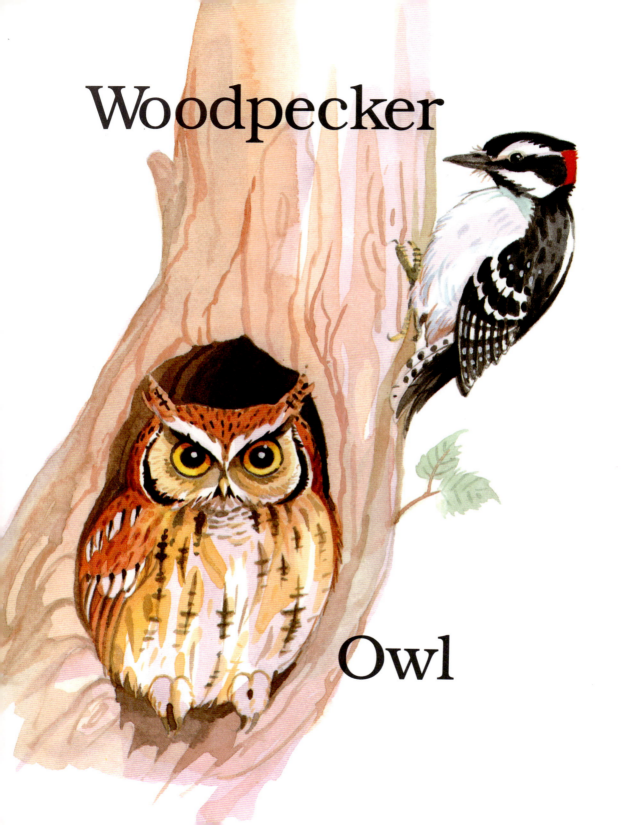

Owl

Pigeon

Parrot

Ostrich

Hummingbird

Bluebird

Jay

Crow

Cardinal

Robin

Sparrow